Pelle's new suit

Elsa Beskow

Floris Books

There was once a little Swedish boy whose name was Pelle. Now, Pelle had a lamb which was all his own and which he took care of all himself.

The lamb grew and Pelle grew. And the lamb's coat grew longer and longer, but Pelle's coat only grew shorter!

One day Pelle took a pair of shears and cut off all the lamb's wool.

Then he took the wool to his grandmother, and said: "Granny dear, please card this wool for me!" — "That I will, my dear," said Granny, "if you will pull the weeds in my carrot patch for me."

So Pelle pulled the weeds in Granny's carrot patch and Granny carded Pelle's wool.

Then Pelle went to his other grandmother and said: "Grandmother dear, please spin this wool into yarn for me!" — "That I will gladly do, my dear," said his grandmother, "if while I am spinning you will tend my cows for me."

And so Pelle tended Grandmother's cows and Grandmother spun Pelle's yarn.

Then Pelle went to a neighbour who was a painter and asked him for some colour with which to dye his yarn. "What a silly little boy you are!" laughed the painter. "My paint is not what you want to colour your wool. But if you will row over to the store to get a bottle of turpentine for me, you may buy yourself some dye out of the change from the money."

So Pelle rowed over to the store and bought a bottle of turpentine for the painter, and bought for himself a large sack of blue dye out of the change from the money.

Then he dyed his wool himself until it was blue all through.

And then Pelle went to his mother and said: "Mother dear, please weave this yarn into cloth for me." — "That I will gladly do," said his mother, "if you will take care of your little sister for me." — So Pelle took good care of his little sister, and Mother wove the wool into cloth.

Then Pelle went to the tailor: "Dear Mr Tailor, please make a suit for me out of this cloth." — "Is that what you want, you little rascal?" said the tailor. "Indeed I will, if you will rake my hay and bring in my wood and feed my pigs for me."

So Pelle raked the tailor's hay and fed his pigs.

And then he carried in all the wood. And the tailor had Pelle's suit ready that very Saturday evening.

And on Sunday morning Pelle put on his new suit and went to his lamb and said: "Thank you very much for my new suit, little lamb." — "Ba-a-ah," said the lamb, and it sounded almost as if the lamb were laughing.

First published in Swedish under the title
Pelles nya Kläder by Albert Bonniers, Stockholm in 1912
This edition published in 1989 by Floris Books
15 Harrison Gardens, Edinburgh EH11 1SH
Reprinted 1994
© Bonnier Carlsen Bokförlag AB, 1994
Translated by Marion Letcher Woodburn © Harper & Brothers, New York
British Library CIP data available
ISBN 0-86315-092-6   Printed in Belgium